Moon And Morning

AMY LAURENS

OTHER WORKS

SANCTUARY SERIES

Where Shadows Rise
Through Roads Between
When Worlds Collide

KADITEOS SERIES

How Not To Acquire A Castle

STORM FOXES SERIES

A Fox of Storms And Starlight

SHORTER WORKS AND COLLECTIONS

April Showers
Bones Of The Sea
Darkness And Good
Dreaming Of Forests
It All Changes Now
Of Sea Foam And Blood
Rush Job
The Ice Cream Crown Skating Races
Trust Issues

NON-FICTION

How To Plan A Pinterest-Worthy Party Without Dying
How To Write Dogs
How To Theme
How To Create Cultures
How To Create Life
How To Map
The 32 Worst Mistakes People Make About Dogs

Find other works by the author at www.amylaurens.com

Moon And Morning

INKLET #87

AMY LAURENS

Inkprint
PRESS

www.inkprintpress.com

Print ISBN: 978-1-922434-27-2
eBook ISBN: 9798201439071

www.inkprintpress.com

National Library of Australia Cataloguing-in-Publication Data
Laurens, Amy 1985 –
Moon And Morning
76 p.
ISBN: 978-1-922434-27-2
Inkprint Press, Canberra, Australia
1. Young Adult Fiction—Fantasy—Contemporary 2. Young Adult Fiction—Family—General 3. Young Adult Fiction—Short Stories, Collections & Anthologies

First Print Edition: August 2022
Cover photo © milangucci via Deposit Photos
Cover design © Inkprint Press
Interior art © Amy Laurens

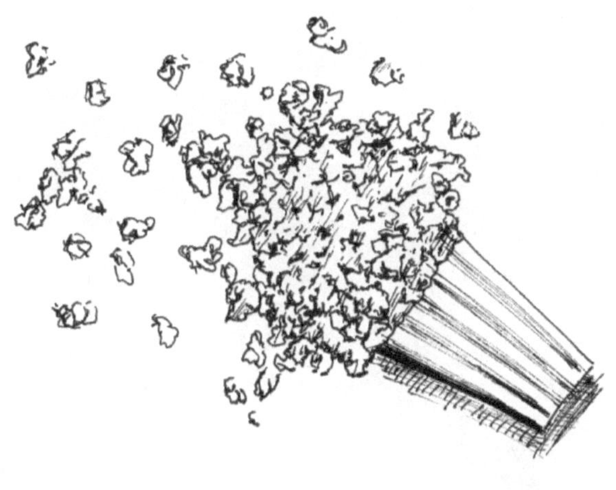

MOON AND MORNING

IT WAS NEARLY DARK, THAT MOMENT when the trees become nothing more than black silhouettes clawing at the orange western sky, all jag-fingered and blade-leafed, when the breeze drops to nothing as the world holds its breath, pausing to appreciate the beauty of the death of another day, the end of one day's way of life.

Around me, the crowd failed to notice. Oh, sure, a few people here and there pointed or gestured from their red tartan picnic rugs or shaded their eyes to watch from their navy blue blankets while they continued the conversation with the people around them; and a whole bunch of people had their phones out, snapping a few pics of the heavenly fire before swiping, cropping, colour-adjusting, filtering, and posting to their social media. The crowd *saw* the sunset, but they didn't *notice* it.

If they had, they'd have stopped with their breath similarly held as the world plunged into sleep.

I stopped. I noticed. But then, it was kind of my self-appointed job to notice things like that.

And, I don't know, I was a morning person.

I had nothing against night-owls—I was kind of jealous of them, to be honest, given as a teenager I was supposed to be one—but it seemed to me that people who were awake to see the very beginning of every new day, who were awake and about their lives while most of the world slumbered... We were used to seeing things that other people missed.

And I was used to noticing things alone.

I sighed, and contemplated writing that down; it would have made a good start to the next chapter of my story.

Once, just once, I thought about how great it would be to not feel like such a freak (unicorn, sorry Dad) in my massive, noisy, sprawling extended family, who spread out now on the five, six, seven or so picnic mats around me anticipating both the annual fireworks, and a subsequent lunar eclipse.

The last curve of sun disappeared behind the mountains, and a moment later the breeze returned, bringing with it the scent of plastic hotdogs and chemical popcorn and all that other standard outdoor sideshow fare, designed for optimal smell and minimum cost, about as real and edible as the notebook covering my crossed legs.

Actually, I'd rather eat the notebook. Sure, the paper's bleached, but at least there's some non-digestible fibre there that's bound to be good for something.

Goosebumps prickled my skin and I rubbed them away, my calves first, then my forearms under the sleeves of my hoodie. It wasn't *cold*, not this early in the year, but the breeze post-sunset was a marked contrast to the earlier warm breaths of the day.

"There!" Someone in the throng nearby shouted, and as one, we swivelled our heads, following their outstretched arm.

Sure enough, on the flat, eastern horizon even more broken by jagged trees than the western, the moon was rising, huge and full, pale silver in the dimming twilight.

Excitement thrilled through me. The last time there'd been a full lunar eclipse with good viewing possibilities, I'd been two. I remembered approximately as much of it as you'd expect from your average two-year-old: a vague sense of sitting on my father's shoulders, curled around his warm head, his dark hair curling through my fingers; a sense of buoyancy, expectant waiting, delight.

But that could have been any one of a hundred shoulder rides, so it hardly counted.

My notebook shifted on my lap. I glanced up as a tall boy brushed past, trying hard not to disturb people as he wove his way through the picnic mats but—hello, my notebook—failing.

"You right?" I said, meaning 'are you alright', wanting to make sure he wasn't going to lose his footing and tumble on top of someone or something.

He pulled a face down at me that I could barely discern in the growing dark, one eyebrow raised in disbelief or disdain or dis-something. "Sorry," he said in that tone that meant he thought I was the one who should be sorry, and kept moving.

"No, I—" I sighed. Too late. He'd already moved on, wending his way past one of our peripheral mats where three of my young cousins hooted with laughter as their dad snapped a pack of neon glowsticks.

Pity. From this angle, in bad lighting, he'd been kind of cute.

The moon began climbing its long arc toward the zenith, and the buzz in the crowd grew. I stretched my legs out in front of me and wriggled my toes, pleased that I'd remembered to pack socks. Early autumn afternoons were t-shirt and shorts weather, but after dark with that bit of a breeze, socks and a hoodie were necessary for comfort.

Beside me, my little brother glanced up. "How long?"

He was the one in our family doing phone service, playing merge-the-dragon or whatever it was he was currently into. I guess I didn't blame him. He was nine, old enough that sitting on the family rug all night was boring, too young to be trusted to wander around in the dark like the older kids, and there was no one in our rather significant extended family around his age. Mum called him a happy accident, born seven years after me, ten years after my older brother. I mostly just called him a brat.

"Um, I think the fireworks are at eight," I said, crossing my ankles, sticking off the mat on the cold, dark grass.

My notebook slipped and I snatched it.

"Why'd you even bring it?" Harry said. "It's dark."

"Shut up," I said reflexively. He was right, obviously, but it was… I don't know, kind of a comfort blanket or something. I hated going anywhere without a notebook and pen. You never knew when inspiration was going to strike, and I'd never forgiven myself for that one time I'd come up with a whole story sequence for my latest fanfic while out grocery shopping with Mum a few years ago—which I'd of course completely forgotten by the time I'd arrived back home.

I leaned back on my elbows and breathed deeply of the cool, popcorn-scented air. Half an hour till the fireworks, then another hour until the start of the eclipse at nine. The weekend couldn't get much better than this.

Twenty minutes later, I was regretting my earlier optimism. A small horde of tiny children had gone rushing past, literally stepping all over my legs; I'd put my elbow in the remains of the hummus dip and now my hoodie sleeve was wet and cold from trying to clean it; and my cousin Ben, age four, had upended his lemonade on my notebook during the three minutes it was off my lap during the hummus episode.

And then, to make things even more exciting, Mum's phone rang. I mean, that's not the exciting bit per se, but it *was* pretty unusual; the phone waves or whatever they were got really, really clogged during Skyfire every year, and getting anything more than a basic text through was practically a miracle.

This was a really, really good moment for a miracle. It was Aunt Izzy. Luna was missing.

Now, a word of explanation about Luna and Aunt Izzy. Luna is two, just about the cutest two-year-old in the whole wide world if you ask me—which people frequently did, since I was Aunt Izzy's number one babysitter of choice—with her gleaming, golden hair and cute little snub nose and huge hazel eyes.

And yes, she's named after *that* Luna, because my Aunt Izzy is one of those Millennials who grew up with a certain scarred orphan boy they all knew and loved, and her son's name is Ron and they have a pair of dogs called Draco and Sirius, and honestly, I don't even understand how she found a husband who let her get away with all that, but hey. I write fanfic for lols and funsies, so I'm not exactly judging.

And I was especially not judging

right now, with a scant ten minutes to the fireworks and a two-year-old missing in the darkness.

Aunt Izzy had gone up to the hot dog vendor to grab a snack for Ron (age six) and Luna had gone with them. Aunt Izzy had let go of Luna's hand for, like, twenty seconds to pay for the hot dog and retrieve her change, and when she reached down again, Luna was gone.

She was frantic (understandably). Had Luna made it back to us? Could we see her anywhere?

We all stood up and peered around, but trying to find a small child in a thick crowd in the dimming twilight was a losing proposition.

"We should split up," I said, frowning. Poor little Luna baby, lost in the crowd and the dark. "Take an area each and meet back here when the fireworks go off."

"Good idea, Rory," Mum said. "You head up that way along the path. Ed," she continued, pointing to my dad, "you take the inland bit there, and I'll go this way. Izzy can take the last quadrant. Harry," she said sternly, frowning down at him. "You sit here on your phone and you *do not move*, do you understand me?"

He sighed audibly, but nodded.

"Not even for the bathroom. I mean it."

"Yes, Mum."

I wound my way down the slight slope toward the footpath, then took off, heading southeast along the shore of the lake.

Every few steps I had to stop or dodge off onto the grass as another knot of people wandered by, talking loudly, laughing and shouting and squealing in the ensuing night. Ahead of me, the moon no long looked quite so fat, but it was blazingly bright and clear.

Bats flew by silently, fruit bats that lived in the parkland that edged the lake, their silhouettes crisp and classically batty against the moon.

Any other night, I'd have been delighted to see them.

Now, though, they just seemed like a bad omen, even though they couldn't really be an omen for anything seeing as this was where they lived and this was the time of night they awoke.

Urgh.

Trees—mostly gnarled eucalypts— began to encroach on the slope of the lawn that led down to the lake, and the crowd thinned. From this distance, the scent of popcorn and hot chips was just a memory; here, the smell of the lake water itself was stronger, cold and algae-ish.

My heart clenched.

Surely there were enough people around that if an unsupervised two-year-old fell in the lake, someone would fish her out…

Surely.

I sped up to a jog, my eyes roving not just the grass on either side of the path now, but the edges of the lake as well.

If it had been a natural lake it might have been okay; there would have been gentle shallows, a gradual increase in depth. But this was a manmade lake, and while I'd heard it wasn't *that* deep throughout, it didn't have to be deep to drown a two-year-old—and the drop-off was immediate, and unrailled.

I could hear my breath, feel it catching in my throat. That cold spot on my elbow burned. But it would be nothing if I couldn't find Luna. I sped into a run.

Please be okay, please be okay.

It wasn't just that I was her primary non-parental babysitter. Our family had a *lot* of cousins, even a cluster of them around my age. But I was the only girl. At least, I had been until two years ago, when little Luna had come along.

She wasn't just my cousin. She was practically my sister.

Hold on, Luna. I'm coming.

There was a small service road running parallel to the footpath on my left now, spindly trees and bulbous shrubs dark, irregular shapes in the night. The crowd sounded far, far away, even though I'd only been running for a couple of minutes, and although the odd couple or cluster of people sat on the edge of the water waiting for the fireworks to start, I had the footpath to myself.

Surely I'd come too far. She was two, and Aunt Izzy had called us within minutes of her disappearing. There was no way she could have beat me all the way down here.

And my side was starting to grab. When I'd eaten a giant box of popcorn in addition to the veritable mountain of cheese and fruit and crackers and dips and chocolate we'd brought to the picnic, I hadn't been planning on having to run less than an hour later.

I stopped, gasping heavily, fingers laced together and leaning on one thigh.

Someone else would have found her. They had to have.

I turned around—

And smacked straight into someone's chest. I drew in a flustered gasp that tasted like cinnamon doughnuts and tried to detangle myself—but I stepped left and so did he, and then we both stepped right, and for a second it was a mess of flailing limbs and disaster.

"Sorry!" I squeaked as we finally disengaged—and my cheeks went hot in the dark.

It was the boy, the one who'd knocked my notebook in my lap earlier.

My heart thudded.

He wouldn't remember me.

He *couldn't* remember me. He hadn't even looked at me, there was no reason for him to remember me.

"What, no precious notebook?"

He remembered me.

Oh, no, he remembered me, and he thought I'd been snarky at him, and I didn't have time to stop and set him straight because Luna, and the fireworks were about to start, and someone else had to have found her, they had to have.

I sidestepped him and ran, northwest back toward the crowd, my picnic rug, and safety.

Someone else had found her. Aunt Izzy, in fact. Luna had been wandering through the little vendors-only carpark that backed the food caravans, heading up the gentle slope toward the main road, chattering happily to herself in mostly-incomprehensible baby babble about the moon.

I reached the family's blue tartan picnic rug right as the first fireworks exploded in the air, a glittering shower of gold and orange and pink that lit everyone's faces like fire.

Luna squealed and pointed, and my heart remembered how to beat normally. I breathed deeply and tucked myself down between Mum and Aunt Izzy, Luna's folded pram at my back. "I ran all the way to the playground," I said.

"Thank you so much," said Aunt Izzy, leaning her head briefly against my shoulder.

Luna grunted and pulled at her mother's arms, reaching for me.

I smiled as green and blue fireworks flashed high in the sky and accepted her happily. I wouldn't have asked to hold her, of course; Aunt Izzy must have been frantic, and if I'd been her I'd have never wanted to let precious Luna go again. But I was relieved for the chance to hold her all the same. I squished her tight for a moment, straightened her little cream coat with the bunny ears on the hood, and set her in my lap.

The fireworks went for a full half hour, dazzling lights fountaining up from the barges on the lake, showers exploding in the sky, love hearts expanding out like the very universe itself high among the stars.

Red, blue, green, gold; white and purple and pink. Glittering light after glittering light, the pulse and beat of the pop music medley they'd been set to pounding out from countless speakers around us as people listened on their phones, on bluetooth speakers, even on old-fashioned portable radios.

It felt strange not to move once they were over. For fifteen years I'd witnessed this autumn spectacle and afterward, there'd been the immediate flurry of bodies as everyone rose, hunting through the dark for misplaced belongings, folding mats and packing bags and heading en masse to their cars, scattered throughout the surrounding suburbs.

So now, the sixteenth time I'd seen them…

The quiet afterward was strange.

Not unwelcome, though; it was quite pleasant to simply sit and absorb the night.

Chatter was slow to restart, and although the hundreds-strong crowd murmured and muttered, there was something subdued about the quality of the sound compared to before the fireworks.

Luna snuggled down on my lap, her head leaning heavier and heavier against my left arm.

I shifted a little, trying to prop the weight against my thigh, and Aunt Izzy reached over to tuck a soft blue blanket over my lap, and over Luna.

I smiled a little as Luna battled her heavy eyes; they fluttered and flittered as she fought desperately to stay awake, but it was a losing battle, and within a few minutes, she was out.

I yawned.

In front of me, Harry glanced up from his phone. "Past your bedtime, princess?"

His teasing was goodnatured: it was a well-established fact in our family that Harry, even at the age of nine, was the night owl, and I was often the first person in the family to bed at night.

I was usually the first person awake too, of course. For me, dawn felt like a magical time of day, filled with fresh air and promises. I did my best work first thing in the morning as the light crept into the world, and I hated missing it; I felt agitated in some sort of inexplicable way when I hadn't seen the sun come up in the morning.

I stuck my tongue out at Harry. Of course I wasn't going to admit that curling up on the mat with Luna right now and joining in her nap sounded like a mighty fine idea.

I chatted with various family members for a while, and watched over Mum's head to my left as the moon grew higher and higher.

Twenty minutes to go.

Ten.

Five.

"Should I wake her when it starts?" I asked Aunt Izzy. On the one hand, Luna was two and would remember about as much of this experience as I did of my first eclipse. On the other hand, it was kind of a special event.

"Wait until it really gets going," Aunt Izzy replied. "It'll take a while. She might as well get as much sleep as she can, she'll be a cranky beast tomorrow as it is."

I snugged Luna gently, careful not to wake her up. "Let me know if you want a hand," I said. I didn't have too much homework for once—I'd just handed a bunch of assignments in and it was still a few weeks until the end of term and the next round of tasks were due—and I didn't mind hanging out with Luna when she was cranky; I knew Aunt Izzy felt less guilty about letting Luna sit and watch TV for the afternoon if she was doing it with me, and I could binge watch the latest high school mega-drama at her house as easily as at mine.

"Thanks." Aunt Izzy patted my head fondly. "You're a good kid. Glad you belong to us."

I tilted my head into the patting.

A cry rang out in the crowd, and people began to point at the sky.

I pivoted toward the moon, and sure enough, a narrow sliver had been carved out along one edge. Something joyful buoyed in my chest, and I settled back on my hands, the pram propping me up, Luna curled on my crossed legs, Mum pressed against me on one side, and Aunt Izzy on the other.

Forty-five minutes later, as the eclipse was nearing totality, Luna stirred in my lap.

I blinked sleepily. Watching the earth's shadow creep gradually over the moon had lulled me into a kind of liminal state, not asleep, but not really awake either.

Luna blinked to wakefulness too, making soft cooing sounds and managing a solid punch in my ribs as she stretched.

Then she saw the moon.

"Moon!" She sat bolt upright, both arms outstretched. "Moon! Luna moon!"

"Well," I said. "It's definitely the moon. I'm not sure it's yours though." I prodded her gently in her chubby cheek, grinning.

"Luna moon." She pouted, stretching harder and waving her hands, fingers flexing as she tried to grasp it.

"Sure, why not. Luna's moon."

Aunt Izzy, who had migrated to the other side of the mat to chat with another one of my aunty-and-uncle sets, glanced over. "Hey, bubba," she crooned.

Luna looked at her mother, then back at the moon, then back at her mother. "Luna want *moon*."

Aunt Izzy laughed in delight. "We named you right, didn't we kid. Well, I'm sorry, you can't have the moon, but you can have your bottle." She fished a sippy cup of milk out of one of the backpacks we'd brought in under the pram and waved it at Luna.

Luna clapped, rose in that delightfully unsteady way of all small people, and toddled toward her mother.

Partway there, she hesitated— "Moon!"—and turned to look at the moon again, now more than three quarters hidden by the shadow of the Earth.

I glanced up at the moon for a fraction of an instant—and frowned. A second ago, it had been mostly dark. Now, I could have sworn that the Earth's shadow was covering only half of it.

I blinked, furrowed my brows... What the heck?

I must have imagined things. The eclipse mustn't have progressed as far as I'd thought.

I looked back down.

Luna was gone.

"Luna?" Aunt Izzy stared at the place where a split second ago, her tiny daughter had been. "Luna!"

Her scream cut through the sleepy aura that had settled over the crowd.

Around, people bolted upright as my parents and aunts and uncles and cousins fell over themselves to get to us, clamouring to know what had happened, where Luna was, where she'd gone, and how.

Aunt Izzy was beside herself, throwing herself to her feet and staring wildly around.

I jumped up to help—and a strange, piercing whistle cut through the noise.

I whirled around toward the food vendor's caravans upslope from us—

and there, maybe forty metres or so away at the treeline behind the caravans, was the boy.

I shouldn't have been able to see his gaze from here, not in this lighting with the moon nearly gone. But I could. And he was staring right at us. At me.

Luna had vanished, and a strange boy who'd appeared now for the third time tonight was staring right at me. He'd whistled for my attention, and now he was crooking his finger at me, beckoning me toward him.

Pulse racing, I detached myself from my family group and wove my way toward him, picking a path through the mats and blankets and limbs of the crowd.

Close up, the scent of the food vendors filled my awareness again, popcorn and fairy floss and hot frying oil. It soured my stomach, and I pressed my hands against my belly to steady it.

Luna was gone—again—and this time the chances of finding her seemed even slimmer, because where on earth had she gone to, and how in the world were we going to get her back?

How did someone vanish, just like that?

As I neared, the boy disappeared around the corner of the popcorn caravan. I followed, heart racing, adrenalin sizzling through my chest, stomach queasy and discomforted. "What?" I said, snappier than I would have if my favourite two-year-old hadn't suddenly gone missing.

"I thought you'd want to see this," he said over the hum of the food vendors' generators. He led me a few steps away, toward the little carpark, and pointed.

There, on the high wall that separated the carpark from the main road, stood a silhouette, a child, precariously balanced, arms uplifted toward the moon.

"Luna!" I shouted.

The boy grabbed me by the arm as I tried to launch into a run. "Shhh," he said. "Don't frighten her, she'll fall."

I hated him for it, for grabbing my bicep like that, for the way his fingers cut through my hoodie, and for holding me back—but he was right. And so, jaw twitching, I shook him free and hurried at a fast walk up the steep slope of the carpark's exit to where the wall met the rising ground level, and I stepped out onto the pale, foot-wide strip of concrete with him right behind me. "Luna," I crooned gently. "Luna, Rory's here."

She ignored me, arms still raised to the moon in front of us—and it was definitely three-quarters eclipsed now. I must have been hallucinating earlier, or had something in my eyes, or...

Something.

"Moon moon moon, Luna moon." Luna gabbled happily to herself, wriggling her fingers, waving at the huge white rock in the sky above us.

I crept closer. *Please don't fall, please don't fall.* I wasn't quite sure if I was talking to Luna, or to me: in the middle, where the carpark dipped down to meet the grass that ran down to the lake, the wall was over a storey tall.

"Luna," I tried again. "It's me. It's me, Rory. Come give me a hug, snuggleberry."

Luna pivoted toward me. "Moon!" she said, face lit with delight as she pointed, hazel eyes wide.

"Yes, I see it," I said, nodding solemnly. "Big moon." I glanced at it. "Well. Not so big right now, but the eclipse is pretty cool."

"Moon hiding," Luna said, nodding back.

I grinned. "Yes, the moon is hiding."

"Luna moon?"

"Yes," I said, inching closer. "Luna's moon is hiding." I reached out, closer, closer… There. My hand closed around her shoulders. I drew her to me and held on for dear life, picking her up, sitting her on one hip, and more carefully than I'd done anything in my life, inching my way back to safety.

When I finally hopped off the wall to the grass, I remembered how to breathe again.

I hugged Luna to me, my cheek pressed against her baby-soft golden hair—and hoped desperately that she wouldn't disappear again.

The boy was staring at us intently. From this angle, in the moderate lighting of the carpark, he wasn't just cute—he was freaking *hot*. Dark hair just long enough to tussle, dark eyes intent and all-seeing, like he was looking right into my soul and had found something there interesting.

I shook my head, and walked toward the carpark.

"Gale," he said, catching up with us—as though I was supposed to know what he meant.

"Sorry?"

"I'm Gale." He held out a hand, presumably for me to shake.

Unfortunately for him, I wrote fanfiction in all my spare time and I knew my tropes. I had four whole pages in my oh-so-important notebook that he'd teased me about devoted to reasons why mysterious strangers got involved in someone's life, and ninety percent of them weren't good.

I kept walking. "Cool," I said. "Thanks for finding her."

Not that he had, not quite, but whatever.

"I need to talk to you." His gaze had not let up, intense and scrutinising—

and not just of me, but of Luna.

"Hold on," I said, shifting Luna to my other hip. I paused on the asphalt at the bottom of the carpark with the hum of the generators muffling the world and dug my phone out of my pocket. *I've got her,* I sent on the extended-family chat group, hoping that this would be another miraculous moment where the message would get through quickly.

It did. Within a second of sending the message, replies began flooding through—relieved and happy emoji, mostly, with a 'Phew' from Dad.

"Right," I said, tucking my phone away and scooching Luna up my hip a little. "Shoot."

He took a deep breath. "She's a meterogician." He nodded at Luna.

I blinked.

"Weather magic," he elaborated. "Well, mostly weather."

"Yeah, I figured that's what it meant," I said. "I just didn't realise you were serious."

He—Gale—shoved his hands deep in his pockets. "Look, you saw what she did with the moon just before."

"I didn't see anything." Why had my grip on Luna suddenly tightened? "She just likes the moon is all."

Gale sighed. "Aurora, you know that's not true."

My eyes widened. "How do you know my name?"

"Meteromagic is heritable," he said, ignoring my question as I pressed Luna tightly to me, arms wrapped firmly around her. "Runs in families. It's usually pretty low-level, though. Not like her." He nodded at Luna again.

"That's ridiculous," I said. "A, no such thing as magic. B, it's an eclipse and this is the twenty-first century, no one believes eclipses are magic any more. C, even if there *is* magic, even if the eclipse *is* part of it somehow, you said this magic is hereditary. No one else in our family is like that."

He arched an eyebrow at me pointedly in the stark white carpark streetlights.

"What?" I snapped. Then, "*What? Me?!* Ah ha. Very funny."

He shrugged. "The name fits."

"Mate," I said acerbically, "I went to school with a kid named River. Didn't mean he could control the watershed." I arched my own eyebrow back at him. "Names are just names. You're being ridiculous. And creepy," I added, my brows furrowing. "Again: how do you know my name?"

"It's not just you two," Gale said, ignoring my question yet again. "Did you not ever wonder where your uncle went?"

"No," I said, sassy, "because it's none of my business."

I turned to leave.

A thought struck me and I whirled back to him. "Wait, have you been stalking me?"

"No!" he protested, hands flying up, palms out in a defensive position. "I was trying to get a second with you alone!"

"Alone? *Here*? Genius plan, stalker boy." I shook my head.

He folded his arms. "Not, like, *alone* alone, just away from your billion and three family members for a second."

"Oh, right," I said. "That makes total sense, try to talk to me away from my family *at a family picnic*. Because it's *so* hard to pick a time when I'm *not* completely surrounded... by... them."

Oh. Okay. So he kind of had a point.

My cousin Neil was even in most of my classes at school.

Urgh.

But even so.

"Look," he said, rubbing at the back of his neck, "I know your name because I was sent to find you, okay? I have meteromagic too, and I was told to come find you and talk to you about it. You're Aurora, right? Dawn? I bet you're a massive early bird, think best first thing in the morning, that sort of thing? Only no one expected *her* to happen, the magic doesn't usually manifest until puberty, she's going to be hella strong, I can't even begin to imagine—"

"That's great," I cut in, breathing a little too fast of air that tasted like cold grass and, here in the carpark, the petrol used to keep the generators for the food vendors running. "But what the hell are you on?"

In response, Gale closed his eyes, head thrown back to the star-studded skies. Feck he was hot. "I'll show you," he said.

I could run. Or walk, at any rate. Walk away and go back to my family and pretend this never happened. I had a feeling, though, that Gale wouldn't be dissuaded as easily as that.

So I stayed—Luna was safe enough for now, happy in my arms as she watched the moon over my shoulder—and eyed him sceptically. "What, something dramatic is supposed to happen?"

"Shhh."

I snorted, but dutifully shhhed.

And shivered. Because out of clear night air, clouds were forming.

The chatter of the crowd began to rise over the humming of the generators—people frantically checking their weather apps, no doubt, because I didn't know about them, but our family had meticulously checked, re-checked, and re-rechecked the weather forecast tonight, and there had been nothing said about clouds of any sort, let alone...

Rain.

It was raining.

Fat, icy drops were landing on my head, my shoulders, the asphalt around me… and one splash-landed on my nose.

What the actual hell?

I stared up at the sky. A small, archetypal cumulonimbus had gathered right over the edge of the lake, spanning maybe a kilometre or so—and it was raining.

"No!" Luna pouted, and I knew from experience she'd be stomping her foot to go with it if she could reach the ground right now. "Moon."

"Yeah, kid," Gale said, eyes still closed, face tight like he was concentrating hard. "In a second."

"Moon."

The rain faltered.

"Moon!"

In an instant, the cloud burst outward and diminished, little wisps spiralling away into the night sky—and the moon, blood red and fully eclipsed, hung gleaming in the sky.

"Ouch!" Gale glared at Luna.

I stared at Luna.

"She did *not* just do that," I murmured.

There was a logical explanation for this. Of course there was.

Sudden freak shower of rain, cloud freakishly disappearing…

That weird moment earlier where it looked like the eclipse had reversed…

Oh. Yeah. There was a logical explanation for all of this—and unfortunately, it looked like the one that Gale was offering.

"Well, crap," I said, studying Luna's adorable squishy face. "How are we going to convince her not to play around with this until she's older?"

"Come with me," Gale said at once. "There's an academy, they'll teach you, and her. They'll teach you everything, I'll teach you…"

I couldn't have raised my eyebrow any higher if I'd tried. "Or, here's an idea, I go back to my family, I tell them what I've learned, and we figure out how to manage it without the help of random stalker strangers."

"You can't tell them!" It was hard to tell in the white light, but it seemed like the colour drained from his face. "You can't tell them!"

"Or," I said, "I could." They were my family, after all, and hadn't he said this thing was supposed to run in families? Besides. There were practically thousands of us. Someone in the family was bound to have an idea that would help. There hadn't been anything yet we hadn't been able to solve.

"This is not usually this hard," Gale muttered, rubbing at his neck again.

"Excuse me, *what*?"

"Nothing."

"Did you just say, 'This is not usually this hard'? Not usually? Not *us-*

ually? How many times have you done this, stalker boy?!" I leaned close, getting up in his space. "Five? Ten? Do you hang out at public gatherings every other night trying to wile girls away with your charms and your…" Well, I couldn't exactly call them lies, could I? Urgh. "Your, you know," I jiggled my chin in lieu of waving my hands, since they were full of Luna. "Stories."

"Three," he said, going a little red in the face. "I've done this three times before, for your information, and yes, the girls I talk to about this are usually grateful I'm here to explain things."

"Usually," I said, "the girls you talk to are gullible." I whirled around and stomped away.

"Is that a no, then?"

I whirled back to him. "What, did I whisper? Of course it's a no!"

"You can't just tell people this!" he called after me. "They'll lock you up, you know. Take you to psychiatrists and have you examined and put you on all sorts of medication, and none of it will help! None of it will take the abilities away. It'll just mean that when the time comes, when they burst out of you without control, you'll have no idea what to do, and people will get hurt."

I cocked my head, eyes narrowed. "Thank you," I said, "for that lovely little insight in your life history."

He reddened further.

"But unlike exhibit A"—I nodded at him—"my family love me."

I left, and as I rounded the corner of the closest vendor's caravan, the salty, buttery smell of popcorn filled me with warmth physically as the realisation of what I'd said filled me with warmth emotionally.

I was right. My family did love me, exactly as I was, and I didn't need anything else.

I wasn't a freak. I was… What was it Dad said? Not a freak, a unicorn.

I nodded firmly as I wove my way back through the crowd of picnic rugs and blankets, small children bedecked with glowsticks and large children playing tag, adults and children alike laughing and chatting and watching the sky.

I glanced up. The moon was huge, and round, and red.

"Moon!" Luna said gleefully. "Luna moon!"

"Yeah, kid," I said, pressing my cheek against her hair again. "It's Luna's moon."

Back at my mat, I deposited Luna into Aunt Izzy's grateful, desperate arms.

I stared Aunt Izzy firmly in the eye. "Aunt Izzy?" I said. "We need to talk."

THE MAKING OF
MOON AND MORNING

Although I've never demonstrated magical powers myself, or had a family member do so, and although I've never watched a lunar eclipse right after a public fireworks display, I love this story so intimately because so much of it is true.

SkyFire is an annual fireworks display put on by the local radio station in Canberra. It's entirely spectacular, and is often used as a testing ground for new and in-development fireworks before their official debut at the Sydney New Year's Eve celebrations each year.

It's held in autumn, my favourite season, and I've attended every year I can remember—even the years where I lived in a different city.

And so, for me, *Moon And Morning* is layered with all those memories: hurrying back to the car in the dark afterward, clutching my parents' hands; the thrill of parking in places otherwise illegal because tonight, on this one night of the year, every person in the city's priority is first and only the fireworks*; huddling under a tarp squeezed elbow-to-elbow with extended family for warmth while cradling my six-week-old son on my lap; my children now old enough to run and play around the picnic mats, festooned and bedecked with glowstick necklaces and crowns that light up their soft little faces in the dark...

The very setting is a palimpsest, layers and layers of meaning stacked atop each other like a canvas that is repainted every year, each scene similar-yet-not-quite-identical, each documenting the slow and gradual shift of my life over time.

How could I not love this story, when it too is a layer of the palimpsest now?

And, with this as the context, how could any story written in this setting not be about family, about belonging, about wonder?

* Of course, this didn't last forever and now the regular parking rules are enforced, but for a while there it was indeed a glory to be able to use the nature strip in the middle of the four-lane road as a car park for just that one single night of the year—a night that takes equal first place with Christmas Eve for its sense of wonder and importance and communality in my life.

Read more by Amy Laurens!

A FOX OF STORMS AND STARLIGHT

CHAPTER ONE

SIX YEARS AGO, I SAVED a fox in the bush. It was only because my dog died. At the time, it felt like a pretty crappy bargain.

It was the first day of autumn—not by the calendar, but by the fresh bite in the morning air, the golden quality of the light as it lit the main road through town in the mid-afternoon.

Sailor was a big, black shaggy thing, something like a Newfoundland, a lively shadow in the golden light, and I was eleven.

I'm sorry to be starting any story this way, but the fact of the matter is, this where it all began.

I'll spare you the awful details. Enough to say that Sailor had got out of the yard somehow, and had been hit by a smallish truck careening down the highway that split our tiny town in two as it blatantly ignored the speed limit.

I saw it happen.

And although I cradled him in my lap as the smell of burnt-out brakes and hot asphalt and turning leaves filled my nose, his giant, furry black head all of him I could hold, there was nothing I could do.

There was nothing anyone could do.

I knew that, but it didn't stop the knot of frustration and guilt in my chest, or the taste of bile in the back of my throat every time I closed my eyes and saw the truck hitting him, again and again and again.

It took years for that vision to fade.

But that evening, only a few hours after it had happened, everything still felt fresh, and raw.

Sunny, my sister, was only nine at the time. She cried for hours, just sobbing like she'd never breathe right again.

I'd cried a little, at the scene with Sailor's head lying in my lap as his big, brown eye stared up at nothing.

It had been mercifully fast, there was that.

And the driver had copped a massive fine—speeding, reckless driving, I think they even defected his truck—and came to visit us later, a big, pot-bellied man standing on our front verandah, shuffling his royal blue cap round and round and round in his hands as he apologised.

But that evening, with Sunny sobbing her heart out on the couch in the living room and Mum and Dad trying desperately to console her as dinner burned on the stove, I couldn't cry, even though the acrid scent of burning soy sauce, scorching brown sugar and smoking rice wine from the marinade prickled the back of my throat and the corners of my eyes.

I was the eldest, and I had to be responsible.

Possibly, if I'd been just a little more responsible, Sailor wouldn't have died.

So I slipped out the glass slider from the family room to the deck while Sunny cried, glancing up at the two storeys of our moody grey house behind me before jumping down the three steps from the rail-less deck to the lawn, and set out for the gate in the back fence.

I couldn't cry, and I didn't want to add anything to an already chaotic and stressful situation inside—but I couldn't stay there, either.

In the gaps between the gum trees to the west, the sky tinged to red and gold at the horizon, the sun sinking slowly into oblivion. I'm pretty sure I didn't know the word oblivion back then, but I knew what it meant, how it felt—and I craved it, desperately.

Anything would be better than the gaping hole in my chest.

And so, because I didn't know where to find it or how to get there, I stalked through the bush, pushing myself until I breathed hard and my lungs ached and sweat ringed me, chasing the way that hard exercise elevated me over my constantly looping thoughts.

Directly above, dark, heavy clouds obscured the sky, and the air was thick, heavy, humid.

Beneath the smell of dry gum leaves and even drier dirt, I could catch a hint of ozone, and occasionally the wind turned cool for a breath as it gusted against my skin, promising a late evening storm.

I strode harder, faster, outpacing the video looping in my mind of the truck's impact.

When the first drops of rain spat at me from out of the sky, I barely noticed. My skin was filmed with sweat, slick and salty, and the peppering of rainwater barely added to it.

That was at first.

But within minutes, it became clear that those first pattering spits had been the early foreshadowing of a storm darker and more intense than any I remembered.

Thunder rolled across the sky, distant and grumbling at first, a lazy background chorus to the rhythmic melody of the rain as it splattered down on grey-green leaves and red-tinged twigs, turning the silvered bark of an old, dead gum to deep grey and making the spiky, tussocky grass seem oddly luminescent in the dying light.

I stood under a grey gum with stains down its trunk that the rain was turning orange, arms wrapped around myself, shivering hard—and for the briefest instant, thought about not going home.

Mum and Dad would pitch a fit.

And I had to be responsible.

I turned, dark t-shirt plastered to my skin, dark hair sticking to my face and clinging to my neck, and began trudging my way back.

The storm closed over properly, clouds rolling over the horizon and cutting off the thin scythe of blood-coloured sunset, making the bush dark and unwelcoming in the premature night.

Lightning flashed.

Thunder cracked hot on its heels.

I jumped—and stared hard at the gap between two ghost-barked trees, where for a second, I was sure I'd seen a pair of eyes.

Nothing moved.

Nothing except the drenching rain, anyway, weighing down the branches that tossed fitfully in the wind.

My pulse slowly calmed.

The rumours we'd all grown up with, indoctrinated since both, spoke of something strange and dark… but in the forest north of here, in the pines, the plantation—not here, not in the natural, native bush.

I shivered.

The smell of wet dirt and soaked bark rose around me, undercut by eucalypt and ozone.

If anything had the power to wash away the hurt inside me, this storm was it. I tipped my face to the sky, imagining that the rain washing over me had the ability to wash me inside as well, and the raindrops splattered hard on my cheekbones, my chin, my tightly closed eyelids.

More lightning. More thunder, cracking over the constant hiss of the falling rain.

And in the distance, something eerie, lifting the hairs on the back of my neck: a strange kind of high-pitched howl, a cry that rang with moonlight and distance, cutting straight through the noise of the storm.

Bolts of lightning streaked across the sky—one—two—three—in the space of half a second, followed immediately by a growling crack of thunder so immense it vibrated in my chest.

I ducked down instinctively into a crouch.

There, in the corner of my eye…

I froze, crouched with my arms over my head.

The strange cries came again—and they were closer.

I stared hard at the place, low to the ground, where I was sure I'd seen something small, maybe the size of a cat.

Flash. Growl.

Rain spitting down.

There. Right there. A small animal, pointy ears, light coloured chin and throat…

The strange, eerie cries came a third time, and my heart pounded fiercely. Whatever was making the noise, it was close. Really close.

The little creature across from me reacted too, flattening itself to the ground.

My jaw twitched.

My heart pounded.

My fingertips bit into my upper arms.

Stay? Go?

Run? Freeze?

The hairs on my neck prickled again and goosebumps broke out all over me.

Cold dread formed a knot in my stomach.

Something was coming.

Something worse than the storm.

I had to get home.

I made it halfway to standing—and a series of strange, awful noises made me freeze again. They were sharp, clacking, squealing sounds, like someone knocking two echoing stones against each other, interspersed with high-pitched yowling...

The creature in the darkness screamed.

I threw my back against the gumtree behind me, pressing hard against it.

My heart hammered.

I peered back and forth in the dark, eyes wide.

Rain drenched down, but my throat was dry.

My pulse pounded faster.

The little creature screamed again—and as lightning flashed, I saw it on its back, legs slashing wildly as something attacked.

The awful, clicking-yowling noises sounded right in front of me.

I slapped my hands over my ears, gasping. Water ran down my face, getting into my mouth, my eyes.

It was hurting.

Whatever the small thing was, it was getting hurt, and I'd seen enough animals hurting today.

Something in my chest snapped.

I flung myself across the ground, leaping a couple of tussocks and a fallen branch before I crashed to my knees.

I crawled closer, desperate, gasping for air through the heavy curtains of rain.

I couldn't see it. Where?

Somewhere here, near the base of that tree...

The yowling screeched right next to my ear. I cowered against the ground, spiky grass pricking my face, wet-earth smell smothering me—but now, there was a strange mustiness too, a cousin to wet-dog smell.

At the next flash of lightning, I saw it.

The creature was a fox—and something barely visible was attacking it, only the gleam of eye or flicker of teeth visible in the gloom.

But the damage was real enough.

The little fox's side had been opened right up, and in the bright, stark flashes of heavenly electricity, the blood was dark, thinned by the constant rain.

No. No more animals were going to die today.

Not when this time, I could do something about it.

I snatched at a branch on the ground that turned out to be more of a glorified twig, and launched myself toward the creature.

I had no idea what was attacking it, but I screamed and waved my handful of twiggy leaves anyway, batting them in the air over the fox like I knew what I was doing.

The horrible clacking cries ceased abruptly.

With one long, low rumble, the rain began to ebb.

I poised, waiting.

But nothing came.

The attackers were gone.

Still gasping for air, pulse galloping in my throat, I sat next to the fox and shifted it carefully into my lap, realising as I tasted salt that I was crying.

I huddled over, trying to shelter the poor creature from the slackening rain, running my fingers over its wiry cheek—over and over and over and over.

"Please," I sobbed, throat tight and aching, chest constricted. "Please. Please don't die. Please."

Please, I prayed to anything that might be listening. *No more death. Not today.*

Not today.

Another gust of cool air washed over the clearing, taking the last of the rain with it—and lifting the goose-bumps on my arms again.

And as it did, I could have sworn I heard a voice. *Neither do I wish him to die now.*

I shivered, drawing the fox close, like it was a stuffed animal I could hug for comfort—its comfort or mine, I couldn't say. I glanced around the dripping bush, eyes wide. The rumours spoke of an evil presence, and I could easily believe that might be what had attacked the fox.

But a voice? No one had ever mentioned a voice.

There was nothing to be seen, and anyway the voice had sounded kindly—and didn't want the fox to die.

Assuming I hadn't just imagined it, of course. Which, half-drowned by grief, the other half drowned by the storm... An over-active imagination seemed highly likely.

Can you fix him? I thought it hard, though, just in case someone really was listening.

Something shifted in my lap.

Around us, the world stilled, dazed from the storm, but also something more, something watching, something waiting, as the bush held its collective breath.

The only sound was the occasional drip of rainwater from the gum leaves onto a fallen log—no insects, no wind, no rustling of leaves.

Just… stillness.

And the fox, who shivered in my lap.

The clouds tore open, revealing a ragged triangle of stars that glittered in the fox's eye as it blinked open and stared up at me.

My chest snagged.

My throat ached from crying, and a headache was forming in the back of my head.

But the fox blinked up at me—alive.

I ran a finger down it again, from nose to cheek to ear to shoulder, all the way down its side to its thick, bushy tail—and the wound in its side began to close.

Laboriously, it hauled itself to its front legs.

I tried to stop it—"No, it's okay, you can stay here, I'll look after you"—but it lifted its top lip to show half-hearted teeth, and staggered away.

As it did, I thought perhaps its fur began to shrink.

And suddenly, it looked larger in the night—as large as a dog, as large as Sailor…

But I blinked, and it was just a trick of the light, because the creature that darted away into the bushes like nothing was wrong at all was clearly a fox, the size of a large cat or maybe a small beagle, and nothing more.

And if something screamed in the night not long afterward, and the cry sounded horribly, horribly human?

Well.

I was halfway back toward home again by then, and I pressed my fingertips to my lower eyelids and prayed my parents wouldn't murder me for getting home so late.

Keep reading! Head to
www.inkprintpress.com/amylaurens/
stormfoxes/fox/
to buy your copy now!

ABOUT THE AUTHOR

AMY LAURENS is an Australian author of fantasy fiction for all ages. Her novella *Bones Of The Sea* was short-listed for the 2021 Aurealis Awards.

As well as a variety of short stories for the Inklet collection, Amy has also written the award-winning portal-fantasy *Sanctuary* series about Edge, a 13-year-old girl forced to move to a small country town because of witness protection (the first book is *Where Shadows Rise*), the humorous fantasy *Kaditeos* series, following newly graduated Evil Overlord Mercury as she attempts to ac-quire a castle, the young adult series *Storm Foxes*, about love and magic and family in small town Australia, and a whole host of non-fiction.

INKLETS

Collect them all! Released on the 1st and 15th of each month.

INKLET #079
Shadows
NEVER LIE
AMY LAURENS

INKLET #080
Here She Lies
LIANA BROOKS

INKLET #081
Perfect
Destruction
An Age Of Unicorns Story
AMY LAURENS

INKLET #082
What Blood
Can Do
AMY LAURENS

INKLET #083
Dancer, Dreamer
Seer
LIANA BROOKS

INKLET #084
As Time
Whirls Slowly
Past
AMY LAURENS

INKLET #085
Far More
Satisfying
Than Hell
AMY LAURENS

INKLET #086
Just
Another Day
In Hell
LIANA BROOKS

INKLET #087
Moon AND
Morning
AMY LAURENS

Some
Impropriety
Expected
AMY LAURENS

NEON SNOW
LIANA BROOKS

Reincarnation
LIANA BROOKS

More Than
Mushrooms
AMY LAURENS

DOUBLE ISSUE
How To Make A Star
& The World Ended
LIANA BROOKS

CAUGHT
IN THE ACT
AMY LAURENS

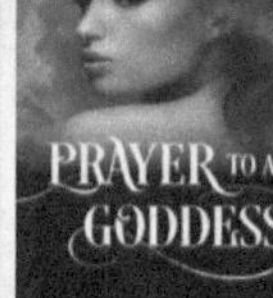

ANUBIS
Has Sent You
Six Souls
LIANA BROOKS

PRAYER TO A
GODDESS
LIANA BROOKS

Love In The
Time Of Corona
AMY LAURENS